In the Ghost Detective Universe:

Novels
(Best to be read in order)

Beyond the Grave
Unveiling the Past
Beneath the Surface

Short Stories
(All stand-alone)

Just Desserts
Lost Friends
Family Bonds
Common Ground
Till Death
Family History
Heritage
Eternal Bond
New Beginnings
Severed Ties

R.W. WALLACE

Author of the Tolosa Mystery Series

TILL DEATH

A Ghost Detective Short Story

Till Death

by R.W. Wallace

Copyright © 2021 by R.W. Wallace

Copy editing by Jinxie Gervasio
Cover by R.W. Wallace
Cover Illustration 10926765 © germanjames | 123rf.com
Cover Illustration 263199440 © Nouman | Adobe Stock
Cover Illustration 262598232 © YAYImages | depositphoto.com

All characters and events in this book, other than those clearly in the public domain, are fictitious and any resemblance to real persons, living or dead, is purely coincidental.

All rights reserved. No part of this publication may be reproduced, distributed, or transmitted in any form or by any means, including photocopying, recording, or other electronic or mechanical methods, without the prior written permission of the publisher, except in the case of brief quotations embodied in critical reviews and certain other noncommercial uses permitted by copyright law. For permission requests, write to the publisher at the address below.

www.rwwallace.com

ISBN: [979-10-95707-85-1]

Main category—Fiction
Other category—Mystery

First Edition

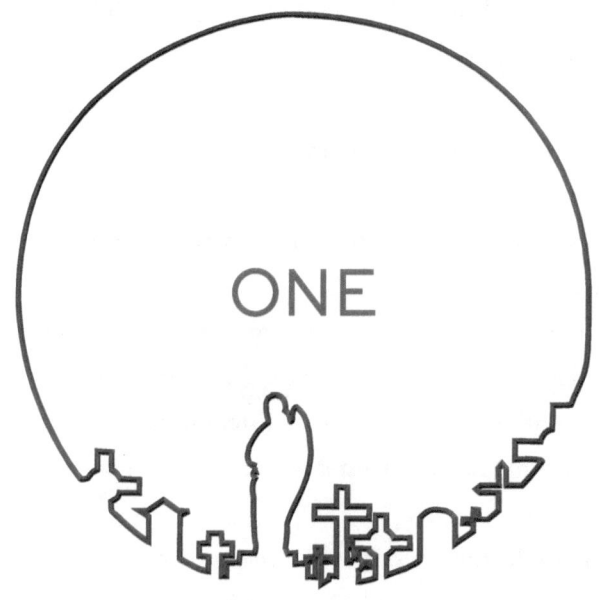

ONE

We don't often get double funerals in our cemetery.

We once had a couple who died in a car crash who were buried together, and once eighty-year-old twin sisters who died mere hours apart. In both cases, the families did a single funeral.

In neither case did any of them linger as a ghost.

This afternoon, when the church doors open and two caskets are carried out, the screams are so loud I'm guessing the ghosts in the cemetery of the next town over can hear them.

New arrivals.

"Jeez, that's loud," Clothilde says from her perch on her tombstone. Never a ghost for respecting the rules of the living realm, her worn Converse slide through the stone every time she swings her legs and her wavy shoulder-length hair blows in a non-existent breeze.

I shove my hands farther into the pockets of my jacket, hiking my shoulders up toward my ears, wishing it would help with the volume.

"Well," I say tentatively. "There *are* two of them."

A snort.

I hope they won't take too long to accept that they're dead. The caskets won't let them out until they've made their peace with it—and until they do, we're stuck listening to the screams.

I cock my head as I listen more closely. "Do they sound… off…to you?"

Clothilde rolls her eyes in true teenager fashion, but she focuses on the noise. "Yeah," she agrees.

"It's not quite the right *type* of screams, is it?" I squint at the advancing caskets as if that will help me figure it out.

Clothilde jumps down from her perch and advances toward the freshly dug grave, leaving me to scramble to follow. Her white shirt billows in the imaginary breeze.

"They're not screams of panic," she says, clearly intrigued now. "They're screams of anger."

She's right.

Where most people—myself included—fight the panic for days on end by yelling for help, and by hitting the casket with all our force, this sounds like we should be expecting two enraged Hulks.

They're pounding on their caskets, but it's not the unrelenting thumps of panic. It's calculated bursts of pure rage—maybe at the casket for keeping them prisoner.

Maybe at something else.

We reach the double-spaced grave at the same time as the group of mourners. Standing less than five meters from the caskets, I can make out swear words, inventive ways in which to kill someone, and just pure, unadulterated fury.

"What the hell happened?" I wonder out loud.

"Dunno," Clothilde says with a smile. "But I can't wait to find out. I'm gonna go listen in on the friends' conversations." And off she goes.

At first, I'm dumbfounded by her enthusiasm. Usually, she lets me do the work on investigating the circumstances around a new arrival's death, and she'll tag along helping me figure things out when she feels like it.

The priest clears his throat, and I snap back to the present.

I have a job to do.

The funeral procession isn't particularly large for a double funeral, and I can only make out one "family" group, so at first, I think we're talking about two members of the same family. Siblings?

The "friends" part of the group seems to average in the late twenties—probably the age of our victims, too.

As I sidle closer to the family members to eavesdrop on anything they might say during the ceremony, I realize there are actually two families.

I most definitely have two pairs of parents—in their late fifties or early sixties—but they're standing together. They know each other well enough to lean on each other.

Our Hulks are most likely a couple, then.

"I just don't understand," one of the mothers—a regal woman with long, graying hair and wire-rimmed glasses—says to her shorter and darker-haired counterpart. "The local police keep saying there are no dangerous currents in the area. But Bruno and Audrey both knew how to swim. How could they have drowned?"

"I don't understand it, either," the other mother replies. "We spent entire weeks by the ocean while Bruno was growing up. He never needed rescuing no matter where we went."

The first mother dabs a handkerchief at the tip of her nose. "I have half a mind to make a scene at the police station downtown tomorrow and insist they send someone to Tenerife to investigate properly."

Seems likely we have a double murder on our hands, in other words.

It might explain the anger.

A bloodcurdling shriek emits from the casket on the right.

I take an involuntary step back. We've had our share of murder cases in this cemetery, but none of them have been this angry at being dead.

I glance over at Clothilde, who's standing between two women in the "friends" section, eavesdropping with a glint in her eyes.

Clothilde, like so many teenagers, has a very short fuse, and although I don't know much about the circumstances around her death, I do know she's very, very angry about it.

"Clothilde!" I yell, not needing to worry about the priest taking offense at me yelling during his speech. "Were *you* this angry when you woke up?"

She glances up at me with half a smile lurking on her lips. Shakes her head.

I stay with the parents until the caskets are in the ground and people start moving toward their cars, but don't learn anything useful.

"You get anything?" I ask Clothilde as we're once again alone in the cemetery and strolling back toward where our own graves lie.

Clothilde shrugs. "They were on their honeymoon in Tenerife. Drowned together in a secluded but calm and not-at-all-dangerous creek on the fourth day. Local police say no foul, but nobody here believes it."

I sit down on the slight mound that marks my grave. My gaze goes to the fresh grave and those *screams*.

"Maybe they *were* killed," I say without conviction, "and they know who did it. That's why they're so angry?"

Clothilde jumps up on her tombstone and sits with her feet dangling and crossed at the ankles. "They'll tell us when they get out."

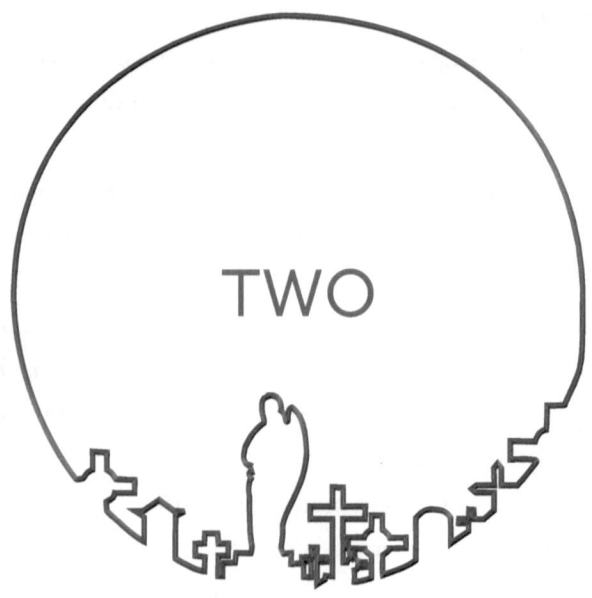

TWO

After two days, the screams and insults are down to being only sporadic.

The good news is, Clothilde and I get some much-needed respite from listening to them, and it probably means their acceptance of their new status as ghosts and subsequent release from the casket is imminent.

Not so good news, or…weird news? They seem to be screaming *at each other* now, across caskets and the small space separating them six feet under.

I didn't even know that was possible.

Now that they're buried under six feet of fresh dirt, I'm not actually able to make out the words, just the general feel.

And they're most definitely communicating down there, with nothing but fury and hate.

These people were on their honeymoon?

༄

Another two days, and one morning we hear a triumphant, "Finally!" as a dark blond head erupts from the new grave.

It's closely followed by a woman's head with long, black hair and a beak nose. "Aaargh!" she screams—at her husband's ghost.

I don't know what happens if two ghosts start fighting—and I'm not particularly keen on finding out. So I rush over to the young couple crawling out of their graves.

"Welcome to our cemetery," I say to them in a horribly fake cheery voice that makes me cringe with embarrassment. "I see you've finally been released."

Yup, horrific greeting.

But it does the tick.

Both man and woman shut up and stop advancing on each other to stare at me instead.

"Allow me to introduce myself," I say, keeping my fake smile in place. "My name is Robert and I've been haunting this cemetery for thirty years already. I believe you are Bruno and Audrey?"

They stare at me as if I just sprouted a second head, but Bruno finally replies, "Yeah, that's us."

The woman—Audrey—sniffs.

Bruno snaps around to face his wife, fists clenched at his sides. "*What?*"

Audrey snarls back at him. "Always talking for the both of us."

Pointing at me, Bruno's practically growling. "He asked if he had our names right. Did I not give the right answer? Are we not Bruno and Audrey? Or are you going to go all feminist on me and force the poor man to call us Audrey and Bruno? Would that be good enough for you?"

Oh, dear Lord.

I have no idea how to deal with this. I wasn't much for relationships when I was alive, and I certainly haven't felt like hitching my wagon to anyone since I became a ghost.

I search the cemetery for Clothilde, but the girl is nowhere to be seen.

Of course, having died at only twenty years old, she might not be much help in this situation anyway.

"There now," I say, trying to sound calming. "I didn't mean anything by the order in which I said your names." I point to the wooden crosses shoved into the dirt at the head of their graves, with their names penciled in. "I simply read them in the order I see them."

Bruno looks vindicated, his lips lifting into a slight sneer.

Audrey ignores me as if I'm not even there.

"And here we go again! I tell you *once* that I'm a feminist and you throw it back in my face whenever you can. I ask you to do the dishes? It's because I'm a *feminist*. I make you fold your own clothes when they come out of the dryer? It's because I'm a *feminist*. Anything that might make you actually *do* something around the house, and you make it about politics.

"Well, it's *not*!" She screams at her husband so loud, I jump back a step in fright.

"It's about *human decency*," she screams on. "About treating me like an equal, a human being. And not your freaking maid and sex slave!"

I seriously consider just leaving them to it.

This is way beyond my area of expertise and things are getting way too personal.

Bruno laughs.

The guy has some balls to have the guts to *laugh* at a woman behaving like Audrey is right now.

"Sex slave?" His voice drips with venom. "You don't think that's taking it just a *tad* too far?"

He turns to me—taking his eyes off the murderous woman not even a meter away—and gives me that look that says, *can you believe this woman?*

Sorry, buddy. Not going there.

"As you may have noticed," I say, my voice not quite as steady as I would have liked, but close enough. "You've become ghosts."

They both look at me like I'm an idiot again, but at least they've shut up.

"Now, as you may *also* have noticed, there aren't all that many ghosts here, despite the numerous graves."

Usually, new arrivals always ask the same questions. This couple doesn't seem to care about anything but each other, so I'm going to answer the questions even if they don't ask.

"The reason for this is that only people with unfinished business linger. So that they can tie up any loose ends before moving on."

Still no reaction other than disdain, so I soldier on. "Do you know what your unfinished business might be?"

"Him," Audrey says, pointing at her husband.

"Her," Bruno says at the same time, with the same gesture.

I nod. Several times. "Right. What about each other haven't you finished?"

Again, they answer at the same time.

"I want to kill him."

"I want to kill her."

My mouth gets away with me before I can stop it. "Well, that already seems to be accomplished, doesn't it?"

THREE

"You think they really killed each other?" Clothilde asks from her perch on her tombstone.

We're at our usual spot, watching the recently married Bruno and Audrey try to kill each other.

They've been at it for almost a week already.

Ghosts can't hurt other ghosts. But they apparently need more time to accept that fact than they did to accept that they'd died and become ghosts.

"I don't know," I reply. "If they did, their unfinished business shouldn't be unfinished, should it? They'd know who killed them, *and* the murderer is dead."

Bruno launches himself at Audrey in what would have been an awesome rugby tackle—if any of the participants had had an actual physical body.

He flies right through her and they both scream in frustration.

"Maybe someone else killed them both while they were swimming in Tenerife," I say. "And their unfinished business is figuring out who it was. The parents seemed convinced there had been foul play."

"Hmm." Clothilde tips her head from side to side as if weighing several sides of an argument. "They were also convinced Bruno and Audrey were 'the happiest couple alive.'" She cocks an eyebrow. "I beg to differ."

I bark a laugh.

"They'll have to calm down at some point," I say. "We'll get the truth out of them then."

༄

It's a good thing we're all dead and don't have anything better to do.

It takes them *a month*.

They quarrel and yell at each other while their family members come and go, while the stonemasons come to install their tombstones, and while the grass slowly starts to grow on their graves.

And then, one day, they stop.

They sit, each on their half of the grave, feet out in front of them, heads hanging, and anger gone.

Exhaustion.

Not physical exhaustion because that's not possible for ghosts, but we're quite capable of the mental kind.

I get up and brush non-existent dirt off my pants. "Wanna come this time?" I ask Clothilde.

"Sure." She jumps down from her perch and skips along the path in front of me like a ten-year-old.

"You could have helped out last time, too, you know." God knows I needed it.

A one-shouldered shrug. "They weren't ready."

Bruno and Audrey look at us through their lashes when we approach, defiant but also resigned.

"I don't think we got off on the right foot the other day," I say and sit down across from the couple. "I'm Robert and this is Clothilde."

"Hey." With a huge smile, Clothilde plops down next to me.

"We're the only resident ghosts at this time," I say. "In addition to you guys, of course. And we'd love to help you figure out what you need to move on."

The newlyweds give me no answer, but they're listening.

"Like I said before, if you're here, it means you have unfinished business. It can be saying goodbye to a loved one, making sure the people you leave behind are okay, finding your murderer. These are just the most common cases. Do you feel like any of them fit?"

Audrey's gaze is flat and her face impassive. She seems completely worn out, and highly unimpressed.

"No," Bruno finally answers in a low but annoyed voice. "None of that fits."

He takes a deep breath and starts ticking points off on his fingers. "If we needed to say goodbye to anybody, we would have done so when they came to visit."

So they *had* noticed, at least.

Second finger. "We've been married for less than a week, have no kids, and our parents certainly don't need our inheritance. Nothing there to tie up."

Third finger. "We were most definitely murdered, but we already know who did it."

I perk up. So there *was* foul play.

Maybe our task is to make sure the killer gets caught.

Bruno folds down the first two and turns his hand to point the less-than-polite gesture at his wife.

Audrey doesn't even bother to move a muscle. "You killed me first," she says.

It's not an accusation, nor a tease. She's stating fact.

Clothilde lets out a peal of laughter, making me jerk in surprise.

"You guys really did kill each other?" she says. "That's priceless. How did you do it?"

"She may have died first," Bruno says. "But she did the deed first. She didn't leave me a choice."

Sitting cross-legged on the grass, Clothilde leans forward toward the couple. You'd think she was at the cinema.

Ignoring her, I level Bruno and Audrey with my sternest gaze. "You're going to tell us what happened. From the beginning. And without accusing each other of murder." I hold up a hand to stop their arguments. "Even if it is true. Now, give me the facts."

FOUR

They were going to spend two weeks on Tenerife for their honeymoon. After a year of planning and a huge reception with almost a hundred guests, they'd deserved some time off.

At least, that's what they'd been telling everyone.

In reality, behind the scenes, their relationship hadn't survived the strain of organizing the wedding.

Once they found themselves alone, with no meetings to go to, no decisions to be made for the wedding, no family or friends to run interference, they'd been at each other's throats.

Not literally—at first.

They argued in their room, to the point where the couple in the next room asked to be moved to a different part of the hotel.

They argued during breakfast, making the hotel staff come over and politely ask them to keep it down so as not to bother the other guests.

They argued when picking up their rental car, ending up with an upgrade because the desk clerk couldn't stand to have them wait with him for the thirty minutes needed to get their chosen car ready.

And they argued on the beach.

This time, they were all alone and didn't have to worry about bothering other people.

Or what other people might think.

When Audrey entered the water to go for a swim, Bruno came up behind her and pulled the string of her bikini top.

Even though there was nobody around, Audrey wasn't the type of woman who appreciated having her breasts exposed, so the yelling increased a notch.

Bruno accused her of not having a sense of humor and that as her husband, he should be allowed to see her bare breasts at least once during their honeymoon. He threw himself in the water and swam away from the beach.

Needless to say, Audrey didn't appreciate the insult, and took off after her husband.

She caught up just before Bruno reached a rickety floating dock that had been set out for tourists to jump from. Launched herself at his head and shoved him under water.

A long and tiring fight ensued, where neither managed to

get the upper hand because they both needed to come up for air from time to time.

Audrey hadn't bothered to put her bikini top back on. She'd just shoved it into her bikini bottom, to put back on once she'd taught her husband a lesson.

During one of their breaks, she realized she should be putting it to better use.

She prepared a knot and the next time they fought under water, she let him get the upper hand and swam down to tie one end around Bruno's foot.

"What the hell did you do?" Bruno yelled as they both caught their breaths.

"You're such a wuss," Audrey countered. "Can't even take some seaweed around your ankle. Seriously, *what* did I ever see in you?"

Bruno attacked again.

Audrey let herself drift below him again.

She caught the end of her bikini in one hand and the chain anchoring the dock with the other.

Tied them together.

She went back to the surface for air.

Bruno didn't.

While she was still grinning in victory, a hand grabbed hold of Audrey's ankle.

Pulled her down.

Realizing the bind he was in, Bruno's anger doubled.

Vowed he wouldn't go out alone.

No way was she getting away with this.

He pulled her down and pinned her to his side while he tried to pull his foot free.

Bruno was a big guy. Strong.

He tightened his hold around his wife's torso. So even though he'd been under water for a longer time, Audrey lost consciousness first.

ଓ

Clothilde whistles. "Man, you guys aren't right in the head."

"You try being angry with someone for the better part of a year," Audrey counters. "And we'll see how much sense you make."

A serene smile that our new arrivals don't know to fear touches Clothilde's lips. "I've been angry for thirty years, honey. You might want to know what you're talking about before opening your mouth."

Luckily, Audrey snaps her mouth shut rather than picking up the thrown gauntlet.

"How come it's not investigated as murder?" I ask. "It must have been obvious that Bruno, at least, didn't simply drown."

Bruno waves a hand as if it's not important. "The bikini top must have come undone, I guess. Wouldn't be surprising once I wasn't pulling on it so hard."

I frown at him. "You don't seem overly upset about this. Don't you want people to learn the truth?"

"That we killed each other on our honeymoon?" he asks incredulously. "Honestly, I prefer they think we're such bad swimmers that we drowned."

A partly playful, partly evil smirk makes an appearance. "They'll probably think that Audrey hit her head on the dock or something, and then pulled me under with her when I tried to save her."

Clothilde giggles. "I actually heard one of your friends say that during the funeral."

"Who?" Audrey finally shakes off her apathy. Her dark eyes glint with anger as she points a finger at Clothilde. "Who said that? I'll *kill* them!"

Narrowing her eyes, Clothilde is no longer smiling. "Honestly, honey, I think you've done quite enough killing already. Leave your friends alone. Not that you'd be able to kill a living human even if we let you try," she adds under her breath.

Audrey hears, of course.

"If you *let* me? Who the hell do you think you are?" She sits up on her knees, leaning forward as if to jump Clothilde. "I'm not going to take any lip from some *teenager* who dresses like she's come straight out of an eighties movie."

I sigh and hang my head.

How could a month not be enough for this woman to work through her anger? I'm going to assume she's not usually this dense.

Clothilde's voice has that eery calm that makes me want to take a step—or ten—away. "I *was* a teenager in the eighties. I died not long after my twentieth birthday, in 1988. Which *means*, I'm old enough to be your mother."

An eyebrow rises and I just *know* I won't like whatever she says next.

"It's not my fault if I still look young and fresh while you look your thirty-five years."

Bruno closes his eyes in resignation and pulls back slightly. Making room for Audrey to come past him when she attacks Clothilde.

But Audrey appears to have learned at least one thing during her time in the cemetery: she can't physically harm another ghost.

"I am *twenty-eight*," she grinds out.

"I. Know." Clothilde enunciates every syllable. "I. Can. Read." She points to their brand new tombstone, where dates of birth and dates of death shine golden in the setting sun.

Audrey deflates, and Bruno and me both let out a relieved breath.

I wouldn't go so far as to say this meeting is going *well*, but I think Clothilde is exactly what we need to defuse these newlyweds.

Her victorious grin at making Audrey back down isn't particularly reassuring, though.

03

"IF IT'S NOT finding your murderers, there must be *something* else holding you back." I've mostly decided to ignore Clothilde's taunts and Bruno and Audrey's reactions to them.

"I want a divorce," Bruno says.

I break into a smile, thinking he's joking, but I quickly realize he's not.

He died three days into his honeymoon and wants a divorce.

"Feeling's mutual," Audrey says. No venom or hate this time. Just fact.

"Excellent!" Clothilde exclaims. "They agree on something. We must be making progress."

"Maybe we could get an annulment," Bruno muses. "That's possible when you ask for it right after the wedding, right?"

"I don't know," Audrey says. "Never looked into it. I was too busy planning the wedding to think about what to do once it was over with."

I share a look with Clothilde and we both shake our heads in disbelief.

"Guys," Clothilde says. "You do realize you're dead, right? There's nobody here to annul your marriage. Or give you a divorce. Besides—"

"Aw, man!" Bruno growls. "This is hell, isn't it? Married to this horror for all eternity."

"Gee, thanks," Audrey says. "Maybe you shouldn't have married me in the first—"

"Enough!"

It's the first time I've ever heard Clothilde raise her voice.

"You guys are unbelievable," she says. "You both need to learn how to shut up, or I swear, I'm going to figure out how to physically hurt you."

They both clamp their mouths shut and stare at Clothilde as if they're five-year-olds who just got scolded.

"As I was *saying*..." Clothilde marks a pause, daring them to interrupt her again. "The marriage vows—which you should remember, having said them such a short time ago—include the phrase, 'until death do us part.' Well." She throws out her arms. "You're dead. *Therefore*, you're no longer married."

Silence.

Slowly, they turn to face each other. Take in each other's gray and ghostly forms.

I can literally see the tension seeping out of them.

Could this be it? Will they be able to move on?

Audrey's focus snaps back to Clothilde. "That's all well and good, but what's the point if we're still stuck here together? This cemetery is really small. I *cannot* haunt this place for all eternity with *him*."

Bruno opens his mouth to retaliate, but this time it's my turn to cut him off.

"Shut it. We've understood you don't like each other. There's no need to repeat it every two minutes."

I let the silence settle for a moment—just to make sure that, nope, they're not fading.

No longer being married wasn't what they needed, either.

FIVE

WE'VE GIVEN UP on talking to Bruno and Audrey together. No matter how hard we work to keep them in line, they end up insulting or screaming at each other.

Separately, they're nice enough people.

Bruno was a software engineer for a large company in the city. I don't understand a word of what he's saying at first, but once he realizes I've never touched a computer, he explains it to me in terms I can grasp. Sort of. Enough to keep the conversation flowing.

"You don't sound like you were a very big fan of your bosses," I say. We're taking strolls around the perimeter of the cemetery.

I suspect Bruno hopes to find a loophole that will allow him to leave. He won't. But he needs to come to that conclusion himself, and I don't mind walking in circles all day long.

Bruno shrugs. "It is what it is. Chances are it wouldn't be any better in a different company. At least by staying, I knew who told me the truth and who lied through their teeth on a regular basis."

"You didn't consider changing careers?"

He kicks the brick wall and shoves his hands into his pockets. "I don't know what else I'd do. I have the engineering degree, might as well use it. Pays well."

"I guess that's an important point." I haven't had to worry about money in thirty years, so I'm actually having trouble identifying with his troubles. "Wouldn't want to starve."

Bruno huffs. "We wouldn't exactly starve. Audrey was an anesthetist and made a lot more than me."

"Right." I frown as I try to put the puzzle pieces together. "So it's a male ego thing? Not wanting to be dependent on your wife?"

He barks a laugh—and kicks into the wall again. Still no give. "Honestly, I wouldn't mind being a kept man. My ego can take it if it means having time to do sports, cook, reading the books I had piling up in my bookcase."

After a breath that borders on a sigh, he adds, "We wanted to buy a house. Get out of the apartment before having kids."

"Uh." I let it slide when he talked about being a kept man, but this…this was projecting into the future.

"How exactly were you going to buy a house and have kids

together if you were getting a divorce?" Or, you know, killing each other.

Bruno shoots me a quick glance, then searches the cemetery to check if Audrey is near enough to overhear.

"We didn't always hate each other."

"You *were* getting married," I say. "I certainly hope you loved each other at some point. I'm no expert on relationships, but I know that much."

A wistful smile makes an appearance. "I proposed on top of the Eiffel Tower. It was so cheesy. She huffed and said she was embarrassed, but I know she secretly loved it."

I want to ask what went wrong, but don't really know the guy well enough.

He offers the answer unprompted.

"We didn't handle the pressure of organizing the wedding very well," he says.

A laugh escapes before I can stop it.

"Okay, understatement." Bruno grins. Then his face falls again. "She turned into Bridezilla. And I...well, I guess I could have done more to help her. I just felt so bloody helpless. What the hell do I know about wedding decorations or which colors go together?"

"Can't help you there, I'm afraid," I say as I step through a tombstone. Spending too much time with Clothilde is making me ignore the physical rules of the living realm more often. "Never got engaged. And was told by my mother at a very early age to only wear navy blue and black because that way I wouldn't hurt anybody's eyes."

Bruno chuckles.

We continue our stroll, Bruno kicking the wall or trying to climb it at regular intervals. I make notes of which graves are becoming overgrown with weeds and which ones have fresh flowers. Some of these graves have been here for decades, and yet, their loved ones come by once a month to deposit fresh flowers, pull out the weeds, and clean the tombstone.

Death doesn't always mark the end of a love story.

"You still went through with the wedding," I say. More a statement than a question. "You could have just walked away. Wouldn't have been fun, but better than an immediate divorce, surely."

Bruno's gaze searches out Audrey, where she's sitting in front of the John and Jane Doe mausoleum with Clothilde.

"Yeah," he whispers.

We finish our walk in silence.

༄

THE NEXT DAY, instead of strolling around the perimeter, Bruno takes us to the women.

I'm a little leery, but Bruno has been very pensive lately, with lots of long looks toward his wife. *Something* has changed.

I'm just not sure if that's good news.

"Good morning," Bruno says as we approach Audrey and Clothilde. "How was your night?"

Clothilde looks like she'd love to make fun of his question, but she holds back with a glance at Audrey.

Could they have made some sort of progress, too?

"It was great," Audrey replies dryly. "Just like the day before, since we don't sleep anymore. No offense," she throws at Clothilde, "but this place gets *really* boring after a while."

Clothilde snorts. "Why should *I* get offended? I didn't make the rules about how this works. I've been bored for *years*."

I'd be offended by her remark, but she's right. Waiting around for nothing can get really tedious, even in good company.

Bruno chuckles and takes a seat at the tomb across from the one his wife is currently occupying.

"Takes some getting used to," he says. "I'm so used to always doing *something*. I feel guilty, I think."

"You didn't seem to be feeling guilty when you let me handle everything for the wedding." The comment doesn't come as a surprise, but the tone has changed considerably since the last altercation the couple had about their differences. The tone is… almost playful.

A corner of Bruno's mouth lifts a fraction. "That's because I knew you had it all handled, *chérie*." There's real affection in the delivery of the last word, and he seems as surprised by it as the rest of us.

Audrey opens her mouths.

Closes it.

Opens it again.

"But I asked you for help *so* many times."

Bruno sighs. Runs a hand through his hair. "Whatever I said, it was never the right answer. Instead of feeling like I was helping you, I felt like I had to pass a quiz. One I didn't even know I was supposed to study for."

Deep in thought, Audrey stares at her husband.

I share a look with Clothilde, where we silently agree to stay as invisible as possible in this conversation.

"I'm sorry you felt that way," Audrey says, her voice soft. Her face has lost the hard edge we saw during the fighting days and the look she sends her husband is downright soft.

Bruno nods at the apology. "And I'm sorry I wasn't able to help more. I guess I sometimes spent more time than necessary at work to avoid coming home to the wedding-planning frenzy."

They stare at each other, doing their own silent communication.

"Guess we could have been better at talking about this back then, huh?" Audrey says.

"That would probably have been a good idea."

Audrey glances around at the cemetery. "Wasn't in our cards."

Bruno breaks out in a smile that completely transforms his face. He goes from looking like a harried man in his mid-thirties to a happy twenty-something newlywed.

"With tempers like ours," he says, "this ending probably *was* in our cards."

Suddenly, and making both Clothilde and I jump in surprise, Audrey breaks out in giggles. "It really was epic, wasn't it?"

I realize I can see the tombstone behind Bruno through his ghostly body.

He's turning translucent.

So is Audrey.

"Hey, guys," Clothilde says gently, not wanting to break them out of their newly found happy bubble. "I think you finally found your closure."

They both frown, not understanding. Until they realize they're fading away.

"Come here!" Bruno holds out a hand to his wife. "We need to go together. I don't want to lose you again."

They pop out of existence just as their hands touch.

"Well," Clothilde says into the ensuing silence. "That was an original twist to a double murder for us."

"Sure was. Didn't even need any outside help." I take a seat next to my friend and bump her shoulder with mine.

She plays along and pretends to be bumped instead of having me go through her.

"I think we did good, though," she says. "We should add it to your non-existent plaque." She holds up her hands as if visualizing it. "Robert Villemur. Detective and Marriage Counselor."

I chuckle. "I think I prefer just 'Ghost Detective.'"

AUTHOR'S NOTE

THANK YOU FOR reading *Till Death*. I hope you enjoyed it!

I'm having so much fun writing these short stories. And it's an immense pleasure to have all of them first appear within the pages of Pulphouse Fiction Magazine. This one was in issue #14 and you can expect to find more of them in future issues!

Did you know I've also written a series of novels where Robert and Clothilde get out of the cemetery and try to solve their own thirty-year-old murders? The first in the series is called *Beyond the Grave*. Feel free to drop by my website to check it out!

You can find a list of my other titles in the next pages.

And if you wish to stay updated on any future releases, you can find the sign-up for my newsletter on rwwallace.com.

R.W. Wallace
www.rwwallace.com

ABOUT THE AUTHOR

R.W. WALLACE WRITES in most genres, though she tends to end up in mystery more often than not. Dead bodies keep popping up all over the place whenever she sits down in front of her keyboard.

The stories mostly take place in Norway or France; the country she was born in and the one that has been her home for two decades. Don't ask her why she writes in English—she won't have a sensible answer for you.

Her Ghost Detective short story series appears in *Pulphouse Magazine*, starting in issue #9.

You can find all her books, long and short, all genres, on rwwallace.com.

Also by R.W. Wallace

Mystery

Ghost Detective Novels
Beyond the Grave
Unveiling the Past
Beneath the Surface

Ghost Detective Shorts
Just Desserts
Lost Friends
Family Bonds
Common Ground
Till Death
Family History
Heritage
Eternal Bond
New Beginnings
Severed Ties

The Tolosa Mystery Series
The Red Brick Haze
The Red Brick Cellars
The Red Brick Basilica

Short Story Collections
Deep Dark Secrets
A Thief in the Night

Time Travel Secrets (short stories)
Moneyline Secrets
Family Secrets

Romance

French Office Romance Series
Flirting in Plain Sight
Hiding in Plain Sight
Loving in Plain Sight

Short Stories
Down the Memory Aisle

Holiday Short Stories
Morbier Impossible
A Second Chance
The Magic of Sharing
The Case of the Disappearing Gingerbread City
The Lucia Crown
Crooks and Nannies

Young Adult

Short Story Collections
Tales From the Trenches

Find all R.W. Wallace's books:

rwwallace.com/allbooks

www.ingramcontent.com/pod-product-compliance
Lightning Source LLC
LaVergne TN
LVHW041717060526
838201LV00043B/776